No Place Like Earth

By Susan Amerikaner
Illustrated by Loter, Inc.

DISNEY PRESS
New York

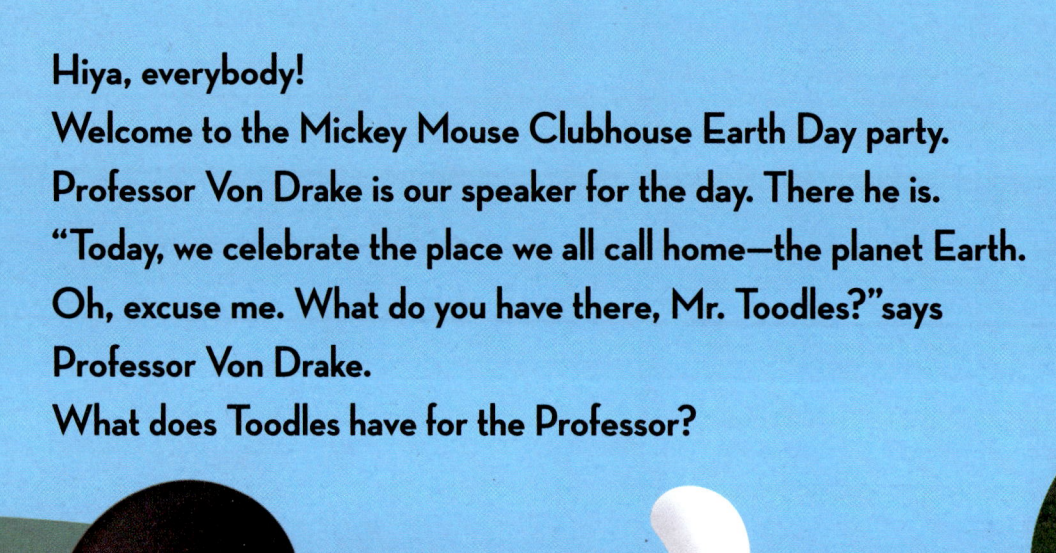

Hiya, everybody!
Welcome to the Mickey Mouse Clubhouse Earth Day party.
Professor Von Drake is our speaker for the day. There he is.
"Today, we celebrate the place we all call home—the planet Earth. Oh, excuse me. What do you have there, Mr. Toodles?" says Professor Von Drake.
What does Toodles have for the Professor?

Yep, it's a globe.

"Aha! A globe is a map shaped like the Earth—the perfect Mouseketool for my talk. Thank you, Mr. Toodles," says the Professor.

Hmmm. The Professor looks serious. He says, "Earth needs our help. It is getting filled up with garbage. We must stop making so much garbage!"

"I know what you mean," calls Minnie.

Minnie says, "When I have a picnic, I don't use paper plates. I use real plates, and then I wash and dry them so I can use them again."

"Right," says Daisy. "I never use paper napkins. I use pretty cloth ones that I can use over and over."

"Gawrsh," says Goofy. "I just lick my fingers!"

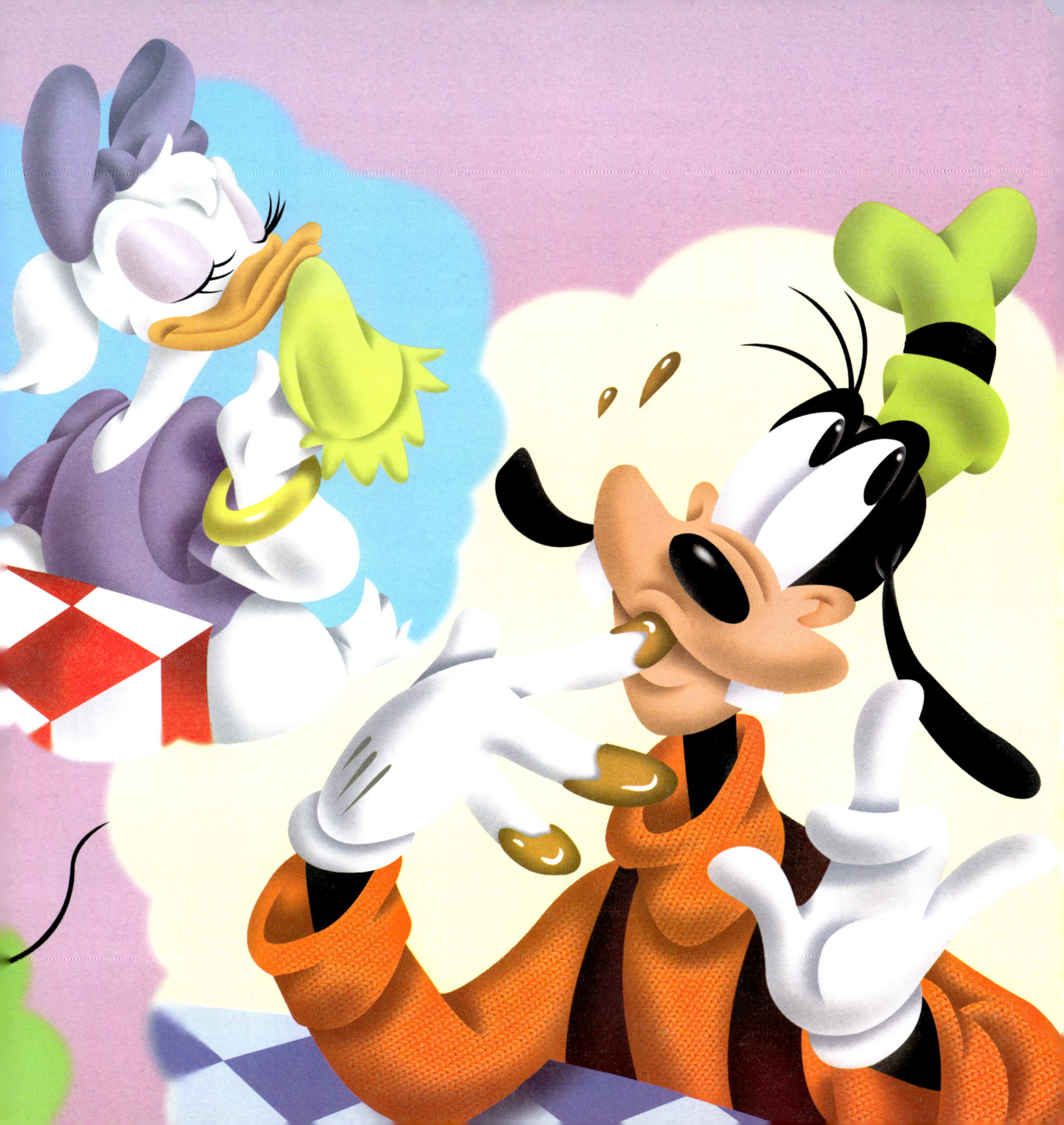

"Er, yes," says the Professor. "Those are all good ways to cut back on trash. As I was saying—"
Now Clarabelle jumps in. "I don't use plastic or paper grocery bags! In my store, customers use canvas bags. Aren't they cute?"

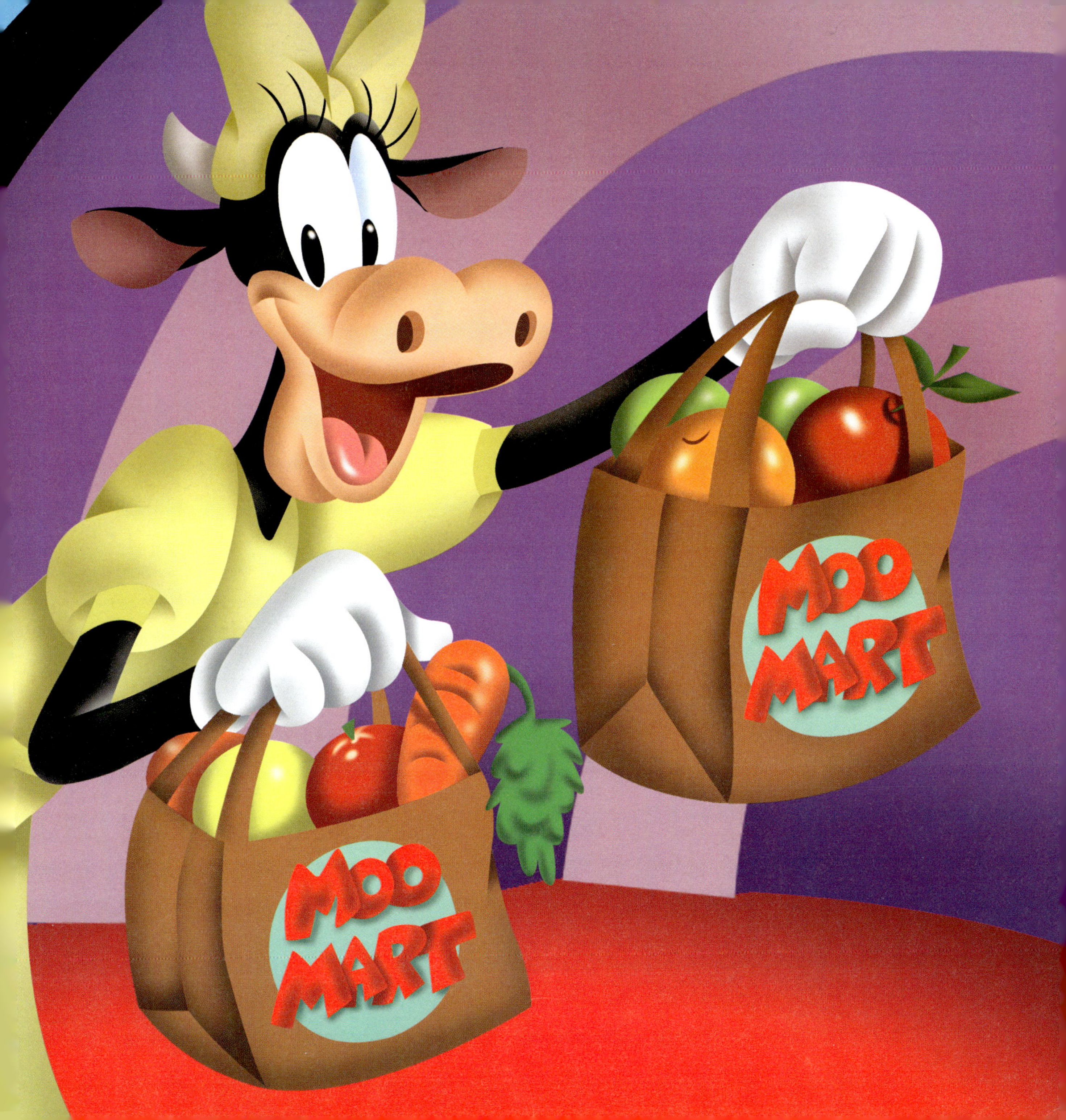
MOO MART
MOO MART

"Thank you, Miss Clarabelle," says the Professor. "Another way to make less trash is to share things. For example—"
"Toys!" yells Donald. "I always share my toys."
"Right," says Pete. "Donald lets me play with his lion sometimes, and I let him play with Clyde, my monkey."

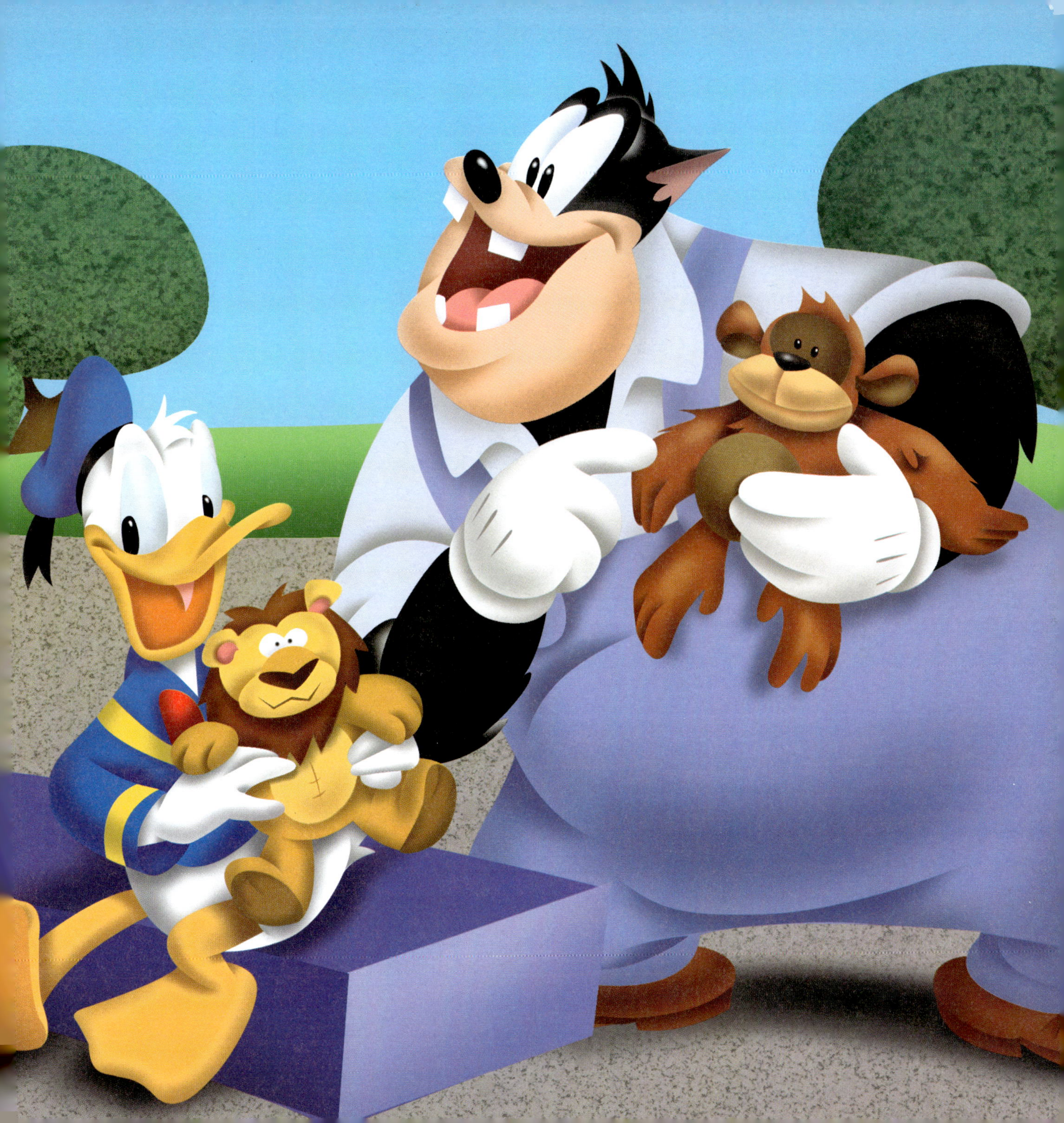

"Very good," says the Professor. "Sharing is an excellent way to reuse things. There are other ways to use things more than once, such as—"

"Oooh, oooh! I know!" It's Pete. He leaps onstage. "When my socks get old, I don't throw them away. I use them to make puppets—see?"

"Oh, sorry," Pete says. "I guess I should wash the socks first, huh?"

Goofy splashes water on poor Professor Von Drake. Good job, Goofy!

"Ach, water!" says the Professor. "The Earth is running out of clean water. What I was going to say next is that—"

"We need to save water," shouts Goofy. "I do that by taking shorter showers. I use a timer, and the bell rings after three minutes to let me know I'm done."

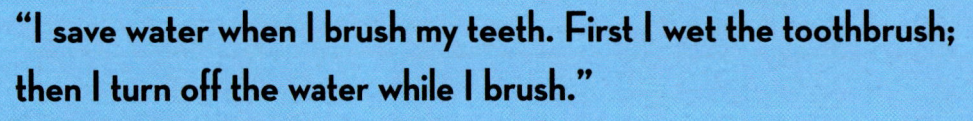

"I save water when I brush my teeth. First I wet the toothbrush; then I turn off the water while I brush."

"Woof," barks Pluto.

"Right, boy! Pluto and Butch save water when they take a bath together!"

Minnie giggles. "And Figaro saves water by not taking any baths or showers!"

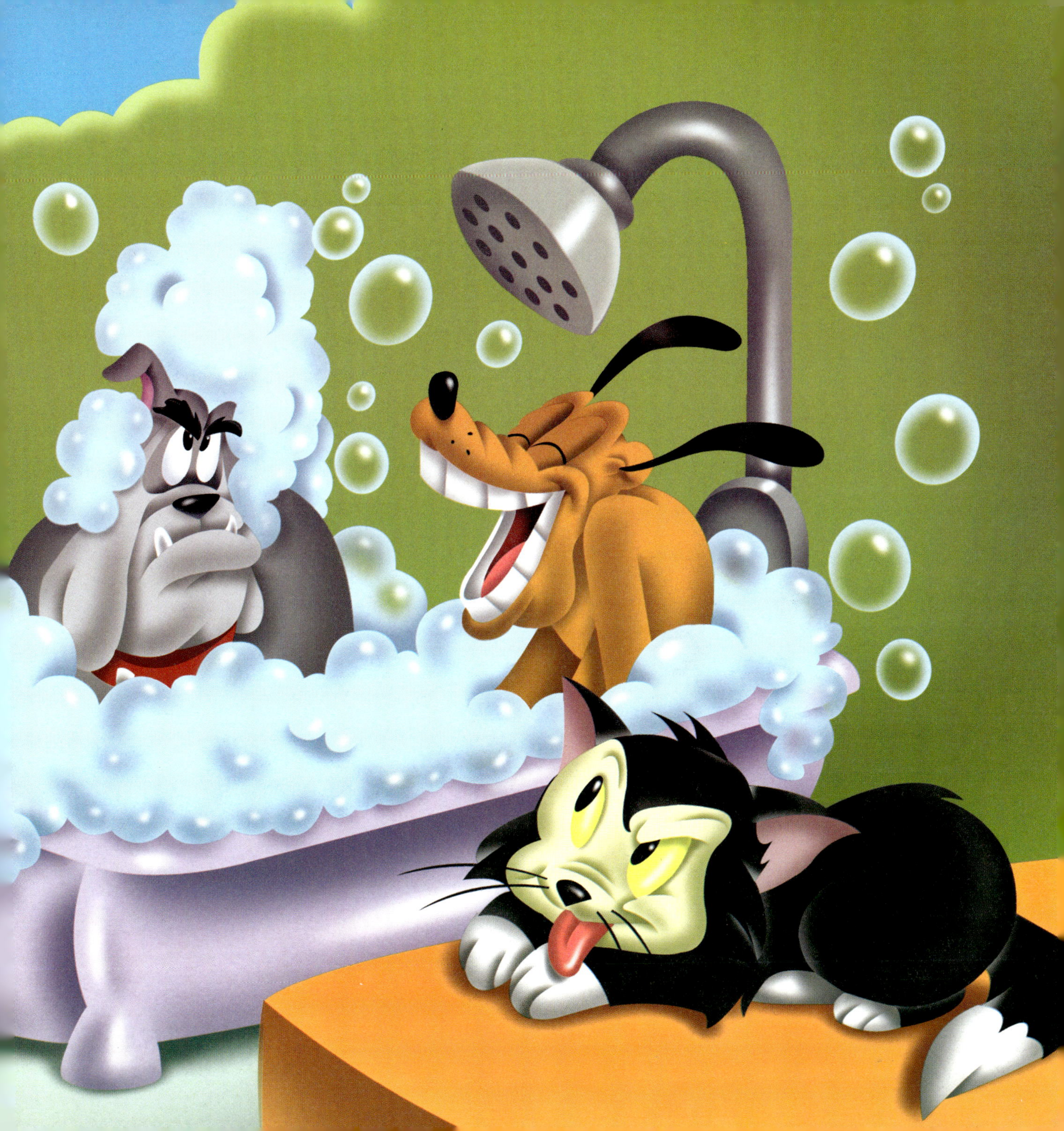

Professor Von Drake sighs. "The Earth is also running out of the fuels to make electricity. What I want to say about that is—" Here comes Toodles again. What Mouseketool does Toodles have? That's right. It's a light switch!

"Very good, Mr. Toodles. As I was saying—"

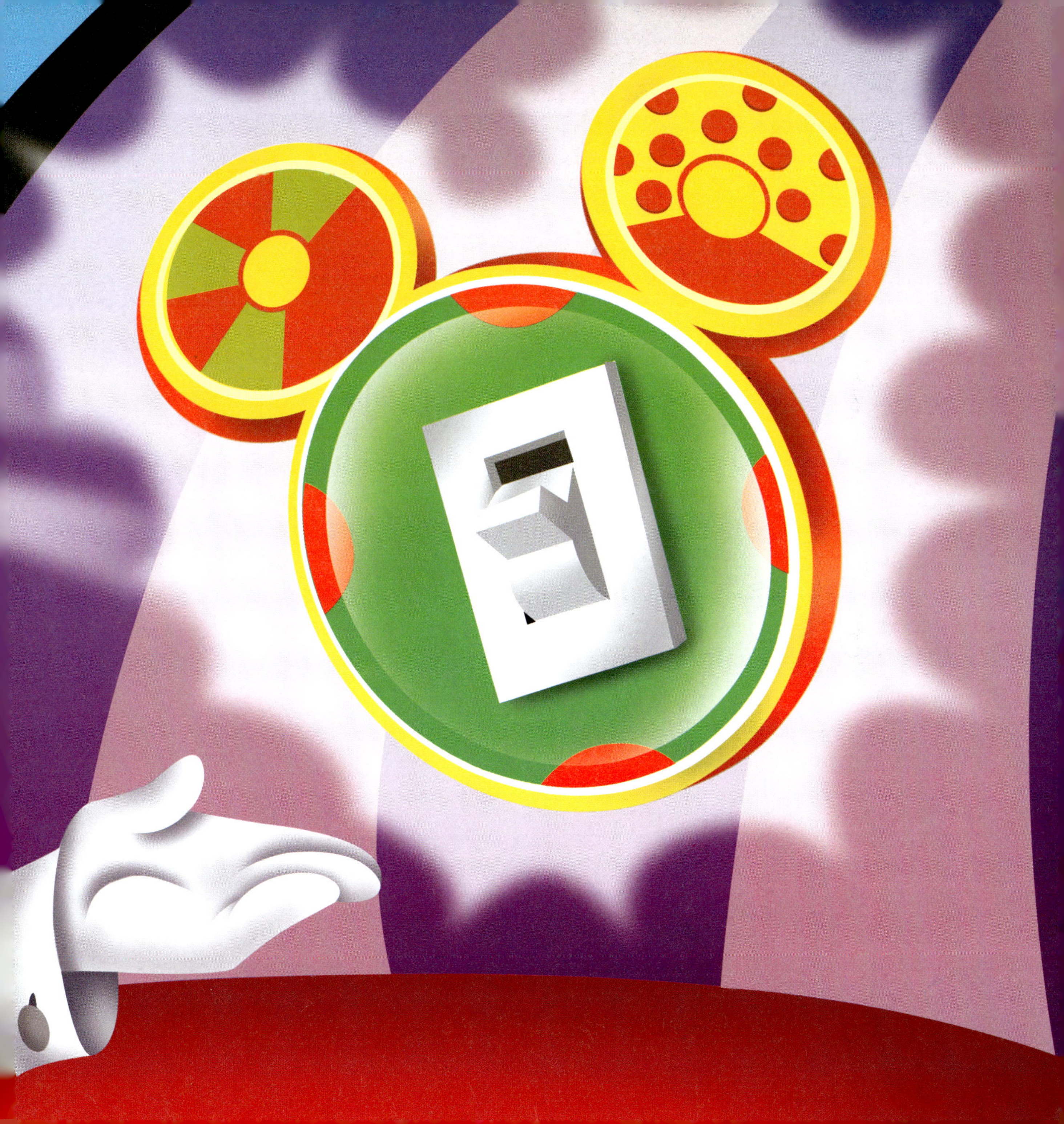

"Turn out the lights!" shouts Goofy. "That saves electricity. I used to turn off the lights all the time. Now I know you should turn them out when you leave the room—not when you come in. A-hyuck!"

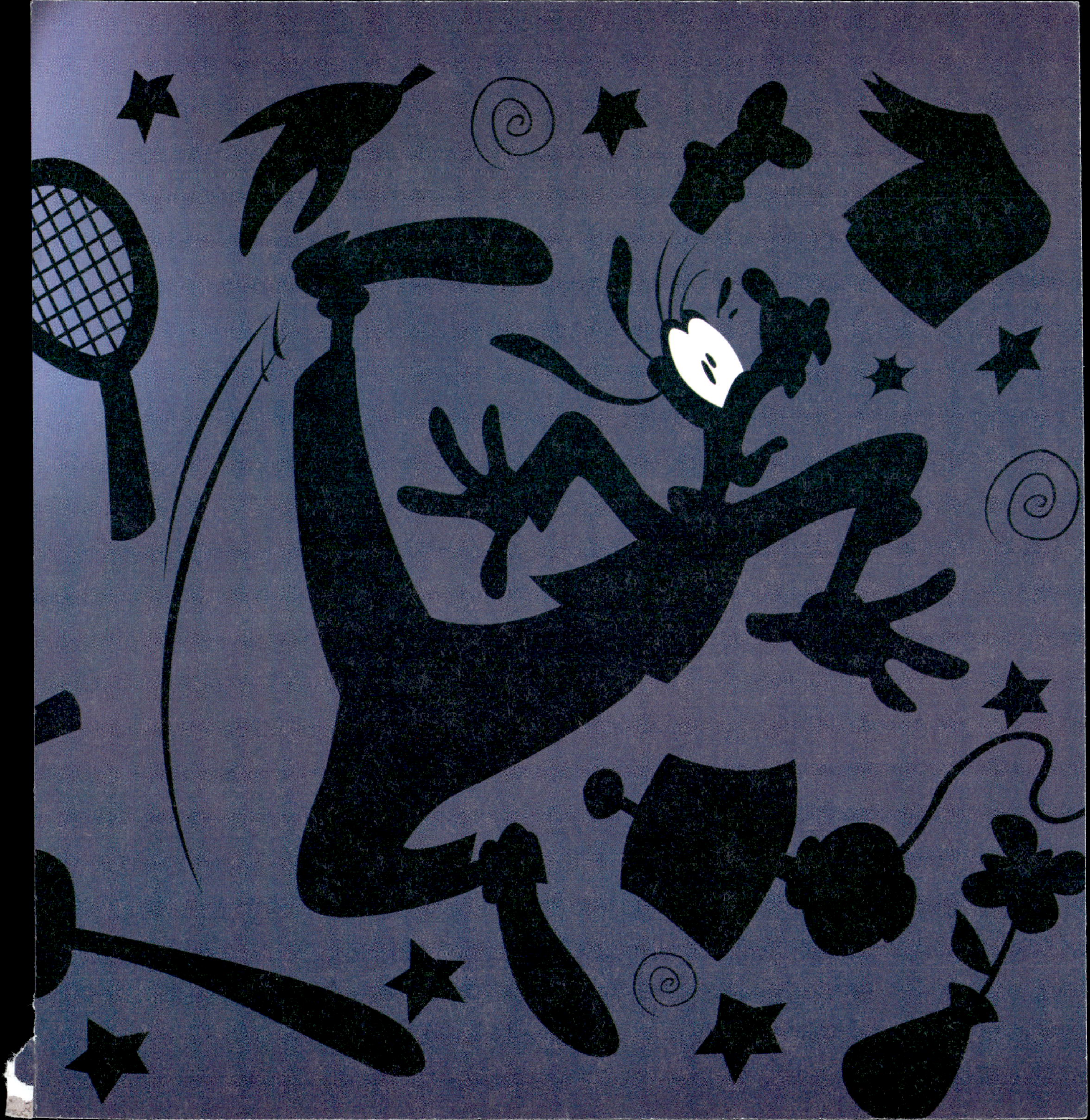

Professor Von Drake says, "Our Earth is also running out of the fuel that runs our cars, so what I must tell you is—"

"Carpool," says Minnie.

"Ride a bike," says Daisy.

"Or a skateboard," says Goofy.

I always say there's nothing like using your own two feet—or, in Pluto's case, your own *four* feet!

"Hot dog! You sure taught us a lot, Professor. Thanks!"
Professor Von Drake says, "You all taught me something, too.
Every day is Earth Day at the Mickey Mouse Clubhouse!"
You betcha! Happy Earth Day, everyone!

Save Electricity!
Turn Off the Lights!

This iron-on transfer can be placed on any soft fabric: a T-shirt, a sweatshirt, an apron, or a canvas or cloth bag. For best results, iron onto white or light fabric. The transfer can only be used once, so be creative!

Caution: this activity requires adult supervision. Only an adult should handle the iron and it should be kept well away from the children's reach. Watch children carefully and do not leave hot irons unattended.

How To Use Your Iron-on Transfer

1. Preheat the iron on its highest temperature setting. The iron must be very hot! Do not use steam.
2. Place a cloth or pillowcase over a hard surface and smooth it flat so that there are no wrinkles.
3. Place the prewashed garment (T-shirt, sweatshirt, apron, or other article of clothing) on the cloth or pillowcase, and smooth out the fabric so that there are no wrinkles. Place the image to be transferred face down on the garment in the desired position.
4. Press the iron firmly over the transfer for 20 seconds in several areas, making sure to cover the entire transfer. Using a circular motion and light pressure, evenly heat the transfer for another 30 seconds. Seal the edges of the transfer by pressing the outer edges of the design with the tip of the iron.
5. Let the transfer cool. Carefully lift the corner. If the design sticks to the paper, lay the paper back down and repeat the entire process.

Note: when washing, turn garment inside out. Wash using the delicate cycle. Use mild detergents. Do not bleach. Dry garment on delicate cycle or hang dry.

There's No Place Like Earth!

This iron-on transfer can be placed on any soft fabric: a T-shirt, a sweatshirt, an apron, or a canvas or cloth bag. For best results, iron onto white or light fabric. The transfer can only be used once, so be creative!

Caution: this activity requires adult supervision. Only an adult should handle the iron and it should be kept well away from the children's reach. Watch children carefully and do not leave hot irons unattended.

How To Use Your Iron-on Transfer

1. Preheat the iron on its highest temperature setting. The iron must be very hot! Do not use steam.
2. Place a cloth or pillowcase over a hard surface and smooth it flat so that there are no wrinkles.
3. Place the prewashed garment (T-shirt, sweatshirt, apron, or other article of clothing) on the cloth or pillowcase, and smooth out the fabric so that there are no wrinkles. Place the image to be transferred face down on the garment in the desired position.
4. Press the iron firmly over the transfer for 20 seconds in several areas, making sure to cover the entire transfer. Using a circular motion and light pressure, evenly heat the transfer for another 30 seconds. Seal the edges of the transfer by pressing the outer edges of the design with the tip of the iron.
5. Let the transfer cool. Carefully lift the corner. If the design sticks to the paper, lay the paper back down and repeat the entire process.

Note: when washing, turn garment inside out. Wash using the delicate cycle. Use mild detergents. Do not bleach. Dry garment on delicate cycle or hang dry.